D1080067

90710 000 422 806

NOR

Caroline Magerl

WALKER BOOKS
AND SUBSIDIARIES

LONDON • BOSTON • SYDNEY • AUCKLAND

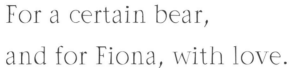

For a certain bear,
and for Fiona, with love.

First published in Great Britain 2020 by Walker Books Ltd
87 Vauxhall Walk, London SE11 5HJ

10 9 8 7 6 5 4 3 2 1

© 2019 Caroline Magerl

The right of Caroline Magerl to be identified as author and illustrator of this work has been asserted by her in accordance with the Copyright, Designs and Patents Act 1988

This book has been typeset in Godlike

Printed in China

British Library Cataloguing in Publication Data: a catalogue record for this book is available from the British Library

ISBN 978-1-4063-9347-7

www.walker.co.uk

Nop
was not plush
in places.

He had no button,

no ribbon,

no scarf or spangle.

Nothing to show where he belonged.

In a place
soft with dust,
he sat and watched
crumbhawks tumble...

over the heaping heaps of goods,
old and rumpled,
at Oddmint's Dumporeum.

Every night,
when all was still,
tealights were lit
one by one.

There were others
working quickly!

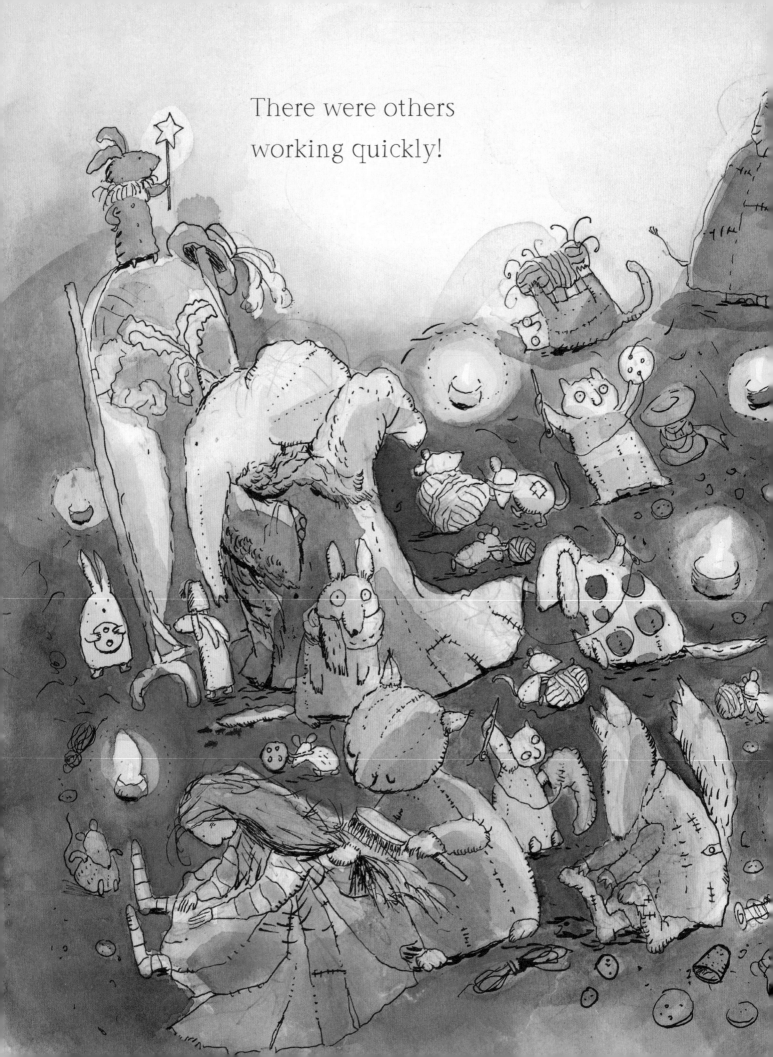

All mending,
    threading,
        beading,
            bedazzling –

buttons,

ribbons,

scarves,

spangles.

But nothing suited Nop.

Soon it would be opening time!
The shelves jostled
with anticipation.

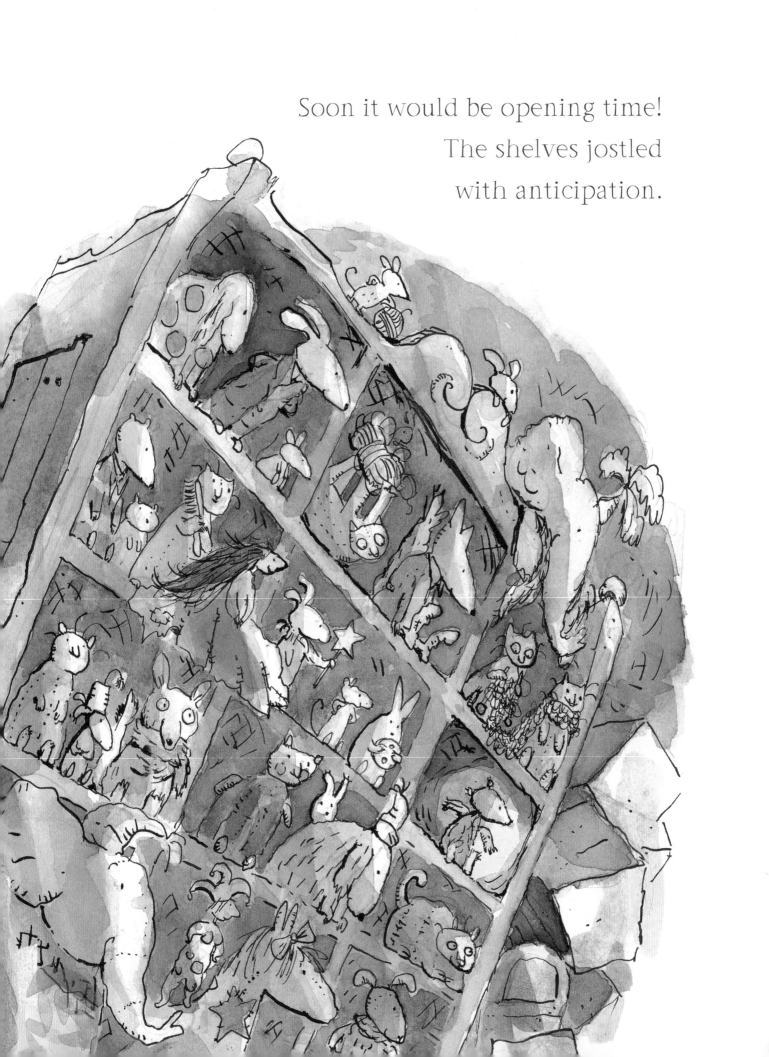

The bell over the shop door trilled all day long.
A crinkly paper bag for each,
with someplace wonderful to go.

Every last one,
but for Nop.

So, he watched the litter tumble.

Until somewhere,
between the top of his woolly head
and his new bow tie,
a thought
landed like a feather.

A bear in a bow tie
can go anywhere,
someplace wonderful even!

By morning,
the thought was a plan.
So with rags and tassels,
scraps and string,
Nop began to stitch.

The wind stole around
the heaping heap
and it harried,
gnawed
and tugged.

And then,
with a puff,
as light as dandelion fluff...

the great balloon billowed
and the twine snapped tight.

The wind seized the balloon
and hurried on.

Nop was soon a speck
in the great march of clouds.

He cartwheeled
and looped,
great breathtaking loops.
Over the jumbled rooftops
for mile upon mile.

Then, far below,
a pocket handkerchief
of green!

Nop held on tightly for a moment
with a tufted paw

then let go.

He whiffled gently down –

through the creepers,
ferns and fronds –
to the delight of
just one
big
butterscotch orange…

friend.